En Quest.

FROGVILLE

Quest of a Frog

Sharla J. Frost

with Ruby Fink

Quantity sales special discounts are available on quantity purchases by corporations, associations, and others. For details, contact the publisher at the address above.

Orders by U.S. trade bookstores and wholesalers.
Email info@BeyondPublishing.net

The Beyond Publishing Speakers Bureau can bring authors to your live event. For more information or to book an event contact the Beyond Publishing Speakers Bureau speak@BeyondPublishing.net

Creative contribution by Ruby Fink, Mike Vreeland and Joie Davidow.

Cover Design - Low & Joe Creative, Brea, CA 92821
Illustrations - Haylee Mae Hunter, Tall Tale Studios
Book Layout - DBree - StoneBear Design

Manufactured and printed in the United States of America distributed globally by BeyondPublishing.net

BEYOND
PUBLISHING

New York | Los Angeles | London | Sydney

ISBN: 978-1-63792-137-1 Hardcover
ISBN: 978-1-63792-136-4 Paperback

Library of Congress Control Number: 2021919329

CONTENTS

PROLOGUE

Far, far away, beyond the Salt Flats of Sitis, over the verdant hills of the Anura Mountains, nestled in the swampy marshes of Luto, was the bedeviled town of Frogville.

No one could say how long the strange inhabitants had lived there, and not many outsiders were willing to risk falling into the quicksand traps hidden by the muck and mire, so no one ever found out. Most curious travelers preferred the royal capitals, Regis and Coronan, where booming prosperity meant plentiful shops, jewel merchants, and patisseries. Others ventured to the Forest of Crystals, glistening with fairy dew, or the Meadow of Eternal Blossoms. Weekly royal balls were held for the people of the land, but no outsider dared to pass over the misty hills of Anura, or enter the musty swamps, knowing they might never return.

It hadn't always been that way. Many, many years before, the marsh and swamp were a crystalline lake fed by a bubbling underground spring. Travelers crossed the Salt Flats of Sitis to enjoy the effervescent water and the clover-laden, moss-covered shores, until the mayor and townsfolk of Frogville began to charge a fee for the use of the lake.

Although the town's coffers grew, so did the local townsfolk's disdain for the tourists who were reduced to spending their last coin on a glass of water. But what could they do? They were forced to pay the fee or die of thirst before they reached their destination.

One day, a wizard visited the town, asking for water. He did not try to hide his identity, like most witches and fairies tend to do, but announced it to the whole town, as he strutted through the streets in his flowing toffee-colored cape carrying a crooked willow staff. "I know what you do. It is wrong and unkind. If you refuse to give me water and continue to overcharge travelers, I will turn every man here into a frog!"

"Go ahead," the mayor scoffed, "I've never heard of you. I wager you are not even a real wizard."

The mayor was correct. The stranger was not a real wizard, but a man who had found a book of spells some years back and begun practicing them — without much success. The townsfolk were so sure that the "wizard" was a fraud, they tossed him through the town gates and locked them behind him, but they heard him bellowing incantations long into the night.

The wizard yelled louder and louder and shook the gates harder and harder until the townspeople could bear it no more and gathered outside the mayor's house "His demands are cruel and frightful," they said. "What shall we do?"

"We'll chase him off in the morning if he doesn't stop," the mayor declared and went to bed.

The wizard had never managed to make a spell to work, but he had always conducted his practice in a placid state of mind. Unfortunately for the mayor and the people of Frogville, the wizard's anger at being expelled from the town brought his magic to life with dire consequences.

When the townspeople awoke the next day, they saw that their beautiful lake had been transformed into a vile, murky swamp, and thick fog surrounded the marshes so that no traveler would want to go there.

"What shall we do now?" the townspeople cried. "We can't charge travelers for swamp water."

Some of the townspeople were dispatched to bring the wizard back so that he could be persuaded to remove the spell. Others tried to clean the waters and return the swamp to its former glory. But days turned to weeks of searching and cleaning until, at last, the townspeople gave up. And the curse evolved.

The mayor's handsome, hale and hearty son was his father's pride and joy. He was intelligent, athletic, possessed of everything required of a future leader. But on his thirteenth birthday, the mayor's son awoke to discover that he was no longer the dashing young man he had been the night before. When he glanced in the mirror, he was horrified to find that his skin was no longer fine as china, and his eyes had lost their piercing ferocity. Instead, he was small, warty, and bumpy. He had turned into a frog!

In a panic, the mayor consulted with everyone he could find. Day after day, he sent messages to distant lands and sent his servants far wide in search of a cure. On the seventh day, he received a reply to one of his letters: "Your son must receive a kiss from a person of royal blood."

The mayor and his son set off at once for the capital where the royal family lived.

They were granted admission to the palace and an audience with the princess who needed a good deal of persuading. At last, when she was assured that her kiss would not obligate her to marry the frog, she took pity on him, bent her lovely head to the gruesome creature, and placed her lips on his warty skin.

The mayor rejoiced that his treasured son had been returned to his former glory and they returned to the swampy village to share the good news.

All seemed well, until one day, another village boy awoke on his thirteenth birthday to discover that he, too, had been transformed into a frog. Then another boy became a frog and another...

The boys' parents realized their only hope was to travel to the capital and beseech the princess for a kiss.

But as the years passed, and every boy in the village was transformed into a frog on his thirteenth birthday, the royal family became less and less willing to aid the citizens of Frogville.

The poor frog boys were forced to search farther and farther for a royal personage who would free them from the curse. Some boys never returned from the journey, and their parents feared the worst. But, from their grief grew a plan. The villagers realized if the boys were to survive the search for a royal kiss, they would need training

Everything they might need to know, from fighting to riding, hunting and tracking, was taught to the accursed children. Every new generation of boys was given this special training in preparation for the dreaded day when they turned thirteen.

CHAPTER 1

PREPARING FOR
THE WORST

"**C**ome on Lily. My birthday is only three days away."

Lilypad Lotus Dillweed looked down from the branch of a weeping willow tree to scowl at her twin brother, Crocus.

"Our birthday," she reminded, sticking her tongue out. "Our birthday is in three days' time, not just yours."

"Yes, but you will not be turned into a frog in three days I will," Crocus pointed out, scowling back. "I have to go on a dangerous quest so that I can become a boy again, while you will be free to stay here and study magic. It's not fair."

"If you want to stay in this boring swamp, study moldy books so that this curse can be broken, and spend the rest of your time helping Mother in the store, be my guest," Lilypad retorted. "I would much prefer to go on an adventure."

"That's not the way the curse works," Crocus huffed. "You think I would work so hard at learning to wield a sword if I wasn't forced to?" He held up a practice blade and swiped at an imaginary foe. "Come on Lils, Master Hopsley says I need to improve or I'll never survive."

Master Hopsley, the village weapons master and trainer, was a perpetually irritated man whose grizzled hair seemed to grow everywhere except his head. His face always wore a scowl, and he never encouraged the boys, but enjoyed berating them instead.

When his sister didn't move from her perch in the willow tree, Crocus sighed, "I'll bring you a trinket when I return."

Lily squinted at him, "Sketches of the places you'll see?"

Like most inhabitants of Frogville, Lily had never left the swamp, but she loved hearing stories from those who had traveled. Crocus was a talented artist when he had the mind to be, and she could imagine the pictures he would bring back.

"I'll try to sketch something at every place I visit," he promised.

After a moment's reflection, Lily sighed, bent her powerful legs and sprang from the branch, landing with a soft *plop* in the mud twenty feet below.

Lily and Crocus had squat torsos, thick necks, oval heads, broad, flat features, and the large eyes and mouths common to all citizens of Frogville. While Crocus was more handsome than Lily, whose head was a bit small and lips a bit thin, both twins were considered beauties.

The villagers of Frogville had become more and more amphibian since the curse. They'd developed long, powerful legs and large feet that allowed them to kick with surprising ferocity and leap great distances. Years of living in the sunless swamp had made their complexions pale and greenish. Their fingers and toes had become webbed, which was useful for swimming or walking over marshy ground. Their fingers and toes had developed tiny suction cups on the tips, making it easy for them to climb trees or rocks.

"I've heard that the skin of people who live outside Frogville is colored differently than ours because of the sun," Crocus said, handing Lily a practice sword and assuming an en garde stance.

"You mean purple or yellow?" Knowing her brother would never attack first, Lily bent her powerful legs and lunged forward.

"No, brown or pink."

Crocus deflected her attack, pivoting sideways so she shot past him.

Lily rebounded against a tree trunk and used the momentum to approach her brother's unprotected side. "What about red?" she asked, as Crocus blocked a side-cut. "Reed told me that some outsiders turn red and shed their skins like snakes."

Reed was a few years older and had completed his quest when Crocus and Lily were only ten. Although he survived, he lost a few fingers while trying to reach a princess who had been imprisoned in an enchanted castle. The princess had stayed behind to wait for a real Prince Charming, but Reed returned in his proper form with a handful of war wounds and endless stories to tell.

Crocus shot out his powerful leg and tried to kick Lily's feet, but she leaped straight up and attacked him with a vicious chop, which he blocked with both hands.

"I think all outsiders turn red if they stay in the sun," Crocus grunted, struggling to deflect the practice blade. He sidestepped, and, as Lily stumbled forward, he tossed aside his fake sword and tackled her.

"The sun sounds very dangerous," Lily gasped, as the air whooshed from her lungs. She landed on her back on the spongy ground, then pushed her brother off her chest with her legs and rolled on top of him.

"It is." Crocus said as he tried to wriggle free. "Father told me he almost dried up while crossing the desert."

Lily shuddered. The citizens of Frogville had reason to fear dehydration. Their skins were susceptible to heat and, if deprived of water for more than three hours, they became leathery husks left by the side of the road.

"You needn't worry," Lily assured her brother as he flipped her over his head. "I tested the enchanted flask I made for you. It can hold five times more water than an ordinary flask and Mother is making you a special cloak that will keep you moist and protected from the sun."

"Thanks, Lils." Crocus groaned as she trapped his arm behind him. He squirmed half-heartedly and sighed in resignation. "I surrender."

"You won't be able to surrender if you're attacked on your quest, Croc," she reminded him.

"I know," he admitted, shame faced. "But I'd rather surrender than let you break my arm. I could have knocked you out at least twice while we were practicing. You were only able to pin me because I withheld my full force."

"Believe that if you choose," Lily sighed, lifting the practice sword. "Would you like to try again with a little more force?"

Crocus glanced at her from under his bangs. "Uhhh…"

An arrow whizzed over their heads and they flattened themselves in the mud.

"Burhead, you oaf," Lily shouted, head down, mud filling her ears. "You almost hit us."

Heavy footsteps hurried toward them, crashing through weeds. A moment later, Burhead's wide, affable face appeared above their heads.

"Good morning, Lily," he said, a slow grin stretched from cheek to cheek. "Please excuse me. I didn't know that anyone else was here."

"Croc's birthday is in three days, mud-for-brains," Lily snapped. "Of course, we're training!

"True," Burhead nodded.

Burhead's thirteenth birthday was only a few months away, but he didn't seem serious about training. He lacked the athletic ability to be good at combat and he couldn't remember anything he was taught. More than once his instructors had shouted at him in frustration, "Do you want to be a frog for life?"

The last time Master Hopsley asked him that, he replied, "Well, I suppose there are worse things."

Lily wondered if Burhead's parents had considered turning his room into a small pond. She doubted that he'd have the motivation to hop out the door. She scowled as she imagined him burrowing in the weeds to nap and coming home for his dinner, which is the way he'd behaved for the first twelve years of his life.

Burhead jolted Lily from her thoughts. "Will you two help me find my arrow? Master Hopsley will have my hide if I lose another one."

"Sure, Bur," Crocus sighed, getting to his feet. "I'm sure it's good practice for something. I'll search the marsh straight ahead. Lil, search to the left. Bur, you search to the right. We'll meet back here when the kingfishers start singing."

They set off in the gathering gloom, wading through the stretches of murky water, using their webbed feet to keep from sinking into the soggy ground.

Lily's route took her toward a small island where she and

Crocus had spent many a summer day playing with friends. Their father had once told her that more than a hundred years ago the island had been part of a crystal-clear lake, the most valuable oasis for miles. Travelers had flocked from all over the kingdom to drink the water. Sometimes she imagined children playing and swimming there: families on checkered blankets strewn over the surrounding knolls green with grass and covered in flowers. Now the area was neglected. An overgrowth of weeds covered the hill and swamp creatures inhabited the water.

Except…as Lily squinted in the fading light, her visions of the past gave way to an oddity in the distance. The island wasn't deserted. She thought she saw a figure at the top of the hill, sitting down with a cloak wrapped around its body, hiding its face in a hood. And by its side, she was sure she saw something that looked like Burhead's lost arrow.

CHAPTER 2

DEFINITELY MAGIC

"**H**ello!" Lily called out a polite greeting as she waded within range of the figure.

"Hello!" came the reply. The voice sounded gravelly and deep, almost like it had not been used in many years. Lily felt her knees weaken. She wondered who this person could possibly be or what they could possibly want.

She squinted in the gloom, trying to make out the figure's hidden features, but she saw only darkness and shadows. "I was looking for that." She gestured to the arrow at the stranger's side.

"Is this yours?" Fingers gnarled like ancient twigs appeared from the sleeves of the cloak, plucked the arrow from the earth, and held it out to her.

"It belongs to my friend," Lily stammered. "I...I'm helping him find it."

The hooded figure extended its hand, offering the arrow. "Take it then, for your friend."

"Thank you."

A loon and a kingfisher sang their nighttime songs.

"We don't usually get visitors here," Lily said.

The hooded head turned to face her. "Oh? Why not?"

"People think it's dangerous," she answered. "They prefer pretty, interesting places."

"Who says that?" The stranger asked, its face still shrouded in darkness.

"Outsiders, or so I've heard."

"Have you ever heard an outsider say such a thing?" the stranger asked.

"No," Lily admitted, "but… those who have traveled outside the swamp have said so."

"It could be true," the stranger murmured. "This place has been a swamp for a long time… but I like to think that a few people still remember when it was something…more."

Lily stared at the hooded figure. "What do you mean?"

"Once upon a time, this place was one of the most beautiful sights in the kingdom," the stranger said softly.

"Until we were cursed," Lily sighed. "I know the story."

"You have heard part of it, but what if I told you there was more?"

Lily looked at the figure. "More?"

"What if, after casting the curse, the wizard was forced to wander the world until Frogville was set free? And the wizard knew of no way set this place free except that he arranged for a one solution—that the boys must each be granted a kiss from someone of royal blood or spend the rest of their lives in the body of a frog."

Lily nodded.

The stranger said, "That is the solution for one individual at a time, but if the kiss were given in true love, instead of obligation, bribery, or request, everyone in Frogville would be forever free." The stranger sighed. "No one has ever achieved that."

"But if someone did," Lily asked, "everyone would be free of the curse, not just the boy who was kissed?"

"Yes," the figure nodded.

"Have you told anyone else about this?"

The figure chuckled bitterly. "Finding someone who will selflessly grant a kiss is very difficult. Your champions have not been willing to invest enough time and effort to make that happen."

"You know…" Lily faltered, "I'm not going to be transformed into a frog, so why are you telling me?"

"You're not?" The voice beneath the hood gasped. "Hmm."

They were both silent for a moment, then Lily asked, "The wizard who cast this spell… is he still alive?"

"Alive might not be the right word," the figure said sighing. "Aware or perhaps existing would be better words to describe him."

"So, this wizard has watched his family, his friends— everyone die—while he remained alive?"

"Yes," the hooded voice whispered.

"Do you think he has been lonely?"

The figure turned to face her, but she still could not make out its features.

"You are compassionate. Empathetic. How interesting. In all the years I have told this story, no one has ever asked that question."

Something splashed in the swamp, either fish or fowl, Lily didn't care. She needed to focus.

The stranger continued, "Tell me something. Have you ever thought of leaving this place? As you said, it is neither beautiful nor interesting."

Lily kicked at a clump of dried mud. "It's my home."

"Still. Why not leave and explore? Then you can decide for yourself if those places are as beautiful and interesting as others have said they are."

"I couldn't do that. My brother is compelled to journey to the outside world, not me. I have to stay here and learn potions and spells."

The stranger seemed to be scrutinizing her. The hood moved

up and down.

"You are in good physical condition. Unless you have an unseen injury that makes it difficult to travel…"

Lily shook her head.

"Perhaps you are needed to support a sick family member?"

Lily shook her head again. "No, my parents are both very healthy."

"Then what keeps you from exploring the world?"

"I'm supposed to stay here," Lily replied, but the excuse sounded weak, even to her. Why couldn't she leave? She could go with Crocus on his quest. He wouldn't need to sketch the sights for her, because she could see them for herself.

"If you were given the opportunity, would you go?" the figure asked.

"I suppose…"

"Well then, Lily," the stranger extended its withered hand, "I hope you are granted that opportunity soon."

How strange, Lily thought. *I wonder how it knows my name.*

As she shook the figure's hand, she felt a jolt of electricity course through her body and caught a glimpse of glowing green eyes staring at her from under the hood.

Then her world faded to black.

CHAPTER 3

TRANSFORMATION

"Lilypad Lotus Dillweed!" At the sound of her mother's voice, Lily snapped out of her daydream

"Yes?"

Ludwigia Dillweed glared at her only daughter, fighting back the urge to sigh. In her youth, her bulbous features and long legs had made her the beauty of the village. But as beautiful as she was on the outside, Ludwigia was brainy on the inside, with an unsurpassed talent for potions.

As soon as she was old enough, Ludwigia established the town's first and only potions shop, selling stink spheres, smoke tablets, and other inventions to families whose sons faced the accursed quest. Her shop was an immediate success. By the time Lily's father, Nelum Dillweed, married into her business, every quester in need of a weapon, a protective cloak, or a hand diversion visited the Potion Pad before setting out on his journey.

"You very nearly mixed the jasmine extract with the stink sphere compound," Ludwigia scolded, handing her daughter the correct bottle. "Do you want your brother's stink spheres to smell like rotten eggs or flowers?"

"Eggs," Lily replied, adding a dash of the correct scent to the bowl of ingredients she'd been stirring.

Her mother nodded, "That's right. We have learned that outsiders hate bad smells. If a quester needs to escape, he can break open a stink sphere and cover his escape while the attacker holds its nose."

"Mother," Lily groaned, "you don't need to persuade me."

Ludwigia frowned. "Do you know which scents are not useful in a fight?"

"Jasmine?"

"Jasmine," her mother nodded, "your brother's transformation begins at midnight," she said, as she stirred a potion that glowed bright blue. "We cannot make a mistake with any of his supplies."

"I know. I'll be more careful."

Lily was expected to join the family business, but while she had an aptitude for mixing potions and casting small spells, she much preferred joining her brother in the practice arena or exploring the edges of the swamp.

At the moment, she was thinking of the mysterious stranger she'd met on the small island. When she'd touched its hand, the world had gone black; and, when she opened her eyes, it had vanished, leaving no tracks. Why had the figure spoken to a girl who wouldn't be going anywhere, anytime soon?

"Lily," her mother snapped again. "Are you listening?"

Lily jumped. "I've almost completed the stink spheres."

"Good, now I need you to prepare these glow tubes." Ludwigia set the glowing blue potion before her daughter.

When shaken, the phosphorus-based liquid emitted an

artificial light for a few hours. Lily had loved playing with the sticks when she was younger, but her mother scolded her because once used, they were worthless, and the potion was somewhat toxic. Still, she loved the calming blue light, and once or twice she'd swiped a tube to use as a nightlight in her bedroom.

Lily sighed. Crocus would soon be off on an amazing adventure, while she would be stuck here, stirring and sorting potions, chopping and mashing ingredients, or selling tubes and vials to questers preparing for their journeys. She felt suffocated by the dull life that stretched out before her—stuck in the swamp, unable to explore the world outside the mist. 'What is keeping you here?' The figure's eerie voice echoed in her head. "What is preventing you from having your own adventure?"

She began to rise from the worktable, then sat back down. She had to help her brother prepare for his quest. Once he was gone, she would be expected to help manage the Potion Pad for her mother and research magic spells for her father. She set a finished batch of stink spheres to the side to dry and began measuring the blue liquid to fill the tubes. Perhaps she would have an opportunity for adventure one day. But at the moment, her future was set in stone.

* * *

Lily had attended many transformation ceremonies, but the tradition never failed to unnerve her. Before midnight, friends and family members of future questers gathered to nibble treats, then joined other flat-faced townsfolk as they silently waited for the clock to strike twelve. As the clock chimed, they witnessed the newest quester shrink to his cursed form. His skin turned darker green and suddenly warty. His eyes migrated to the top of his head and his mouth widened into that of a frog.

When his transformation was complete, the village elder scooped him up and declared him the newest champion, then took him to a moist, safe place to rest for the night. In the morning, his family equipped him with enchanted supplies and sent him on his way. It had been the same for as long as Lily could remember, for as long as her parents could remember, and her parents' parents.

Lily wandered around her home, chatting with friends and family, while her mother served her special leek and mushroom pasties, but she could barely eat. She glanced at the clock. Only twenty minutes until midnight.

She found her twin brother hiding in a dim alcove. His skin had taken on a haunting pallor.

"Hey," she murmured, passing him a pastie.

"Hey." Crocus took the offering and turned it over in his hands, staring off into the distance.

"You performed bravely in our sparring match the other day," she said.

Crocus shrugged. "I could have performed better, but thank you. During our last class, Master Hopsley said that my technique was adequate."

"High praise coming from him." Lily gave her brother an encouraging nudge as they sat in the darkness. "I made a new set of stink spheres for you," "she said. Father enchanted them. Your equipment is the best of the best."

"I know."

"Mother double-checked your cloak and water supplies. You'll be so protected during your journey, you won't have any good stories to tell."

"Let's hope so," Crocus mumbled.

"Remember to bring me pictures, so I can pretend I was with you."

"I will."

Silence. Tears welled and spilled down both twins' cheeks. In the thirteen years of their lives, they had played, laughed, sparred, and cried together. They had never been apart before.

"Crocus," Lily whispered, "I'll miss you."

He slid his hand over hers and squeezed, "I'll miss you, too."

They heard their father, Nelum, in the next room announce, "Friends. Family. It's nearly time."

"Time to go." Crocus released Lily's hand, got to his feet,

and headed for the living room. Lily followed. The assembled guests found seats on moss-covered chairs encircling Crocus, who fidgeted, scratched his knee, and then sat on his thumbs and jiggled his legs.

Lily felt a pang of sympathy for her brother. He hated being the center of attention, and soon everyone would witness the start of the perilous journey he had been preparing for all his life.

The first chime echoed through the house.

"So it begins," Ludwigia murmured and grasped Nelum's hand. The second chime sounded. All eyes turned to Crocus, who was looking a little paler than usual, but had not begun to change.

Something must be wrong with the curse, Lily thought. As the clock continued to chime, Crocus seemed to grow bigger and bigger.

Lily's felt a sudden tingle all over, as though a million tiny pins and needles were spreading through her body. Her skin tightened like the buds of a flower closing for the night. Glancing over, she saw that Crocus had grown as tall as a tree. *How odd,* she thought. In all the transformation ceremonies she had attended, the quester had never before grown taller.

Lily's mother loomed over her, obstructing her field of vision. "Lily!" she shrieked. "You've become a frog!"

CHAPTER 4

A NEW CHAMPION

Lily's father fretted, "Crocus should have transformed, not Lily. Is this a new variant of the curse? Isn't it enough we've had to put our sons in danger? Are we now forced to send our daughters off, as well?"

"Calm down, my slimy slug," Ludwigia said.

"Calm down? My little froglet has not been trained for this quest!"

"That's not entirely true," Crocus whispered. Of all the assembled guests, he seemed to be the least shaken. "Lily has been helping me practice and she has accompanied me on some of my wilderness activities." He glanced at his sister who had been deposited on a small bed of damp moss. "She's as good at fighting and surviving as I am, if not better."

Lily snorted as best she could through her frog nose. "I can fight rings around you!"

"Why is this happening?" Nelum teetered on the verge of hysterics.

Ludwigia turned to her mother, Nucifera, who was one of the eldest villagers. "Mother, has anything of this nature happened before?" Her voice was shaking.

Nucifera closed her eyes and considered. She was a small, wrinkled woman, covered in warts, with a squat, flattish nose, but her memory was sharp.

"Once," she replied "when I was barely old enough to attend a transformation ceremony, two brothers, also twins, were preparing for their quest. At the stroke of twelve, one of the boys transformed, but the other did not. Perhaps the magic in the curse can only affect one child at a time." She looked first at Lily, then Crocus. "Remind me. Which child was born first?"

"Lily, though not by much," Ludwigia replied.

"Perhaps that distinction has played a part in confusing this curse, as well. Before, it was also the eldest twin who transformed."

"But...but..." Nelum was still bewildered. "Lily is not prepared. She can't leave tomorrow."

"The rules are clear," his mother-in-law said. "Once the child transforms, the quester must set off immediately to remove the curse."

Nelum pleaded. "But we must keep her here a little while longer to complete her training."

Nucifera shook her head. "To do so would mean that others in the village could stay behind, as well. The Dillweed family must set a good example by respecting tradition, no matter the circumstances."

Lily was sure she saw a flicker of pity in her grandmother's eyes.

"Whatever she has learned, will have to be enough," Nucifera said.

"Mother. Father," Lily spoke as soothingly as she could as her parents wept. "Please don't fret. Crocus is right. I have learned a lot while helping him." It felt strange to speak with her new mouth. "I will depart on my quest and come home to you."

"Brave words, from the mouth of a froglet," Nucifera murmured, respect in her eyes. She lifted Lily gently from the moss bed and turned to Ludwigia. "With your permission, daughter, the ceremony will continue."

She held Lily above the heads of the assembled crowd so they all could see her.

"I present Frogville's newest champion." Her voice could be heard in every corner of the room. "Lilypad Lotus Dillweed. May her quest be victorious!"

* * *

Later, as Lily lay on her improvised bed of moss, she remembered the stranger's words.

'If you were given the opportunity, would you go?'

Now it seemed she had no choice.

CHAPTER 5

THE JOURNEY BEGINS

Dawn rose over Frogville as it always had. The mist and gloom of the swamp lightened from pitch black to grey. The marsh birds bellowed their morning songs.

Lily awoke feeling strange. Her bed seemed larger. She was surrounded by moss and the furniture was huge. She reached out to rub her eyes and was confronted by a small, green hand with knobby digits. She screamed a hoarse, croaking sound. She had forgotten that she was a frog.

The events of the night before rushed back as she looked down at her body.

"Good morning, my little froglet," Ludwigia greeted her.

Her scream had brought her parents rushing to her room, with a sleepy Crocus trailing behind.

Nelum placed a small box on her moss bed and attempted a smile. "How are you feeling?"

"Strange." Lily attempted to move her new limbs. "A little stiff. And dry."

"Soak in this for a while," her mother said, placing a bowl of water on the mossy bed. "You must be hydrated before you begin your journey."

Lily bent over the bowl to drink, but Nelum reminded her, "Your new skin will soak up the water now." She was still struggling with the awkwardness of her limbs, but she managed to clamber into the bowl.

"Be careful. You can dry out very quickly," her father said.

Lily sighed with relief as she splashed in the bowl. She'd heard this speech many times while Nelum prepared Crocus for his quest. Now it was strange to hear him saying those words to her.

Ludwigia held out the small, olive-green cloak Lily had helped her make for Crocus. She had infused it with spells to protect him from harm. The outer fabric was soft, almost slick, like new leaves, but the cloak was lined in damp moss to keep the wearer hydrated. Lily knew it would remain damp for at least a day, no matter the heat, before it needed to be soaked in water. She saw Crocus watching her with a look of pity. Or was it relief? Perhaps envy? She took the coat from her mother, slipped it on, and felt its cool weight settle around her shoulders.

Crocus tried to smile. "You wear it well, Lils. Green is a flattering color."

Lily looked down at her new body, her bumpy arms, and legs. "I'm all green now, you dolt." She tried to lighten the mood.

Crocus laughed a little. "I want to give you this," he said and placed a long, rectangular object wrapped in woven reeds on the mossy bed.

Lily hopped out of the water bowl and pulled back the covering. Her throat constricted. It was her brother's most treasured weapon, Splinter, the sword he made and enchanted for his quest. It was shorter than the average sword, but the blade was razor-sharp and the hand-grip of woven reeds was masterfully crafted.

"I added this last night." Crocus pointed to a small lily flower he had engraved on the hilt of the crossbar.

Lily shook her head. "Crocus, I can't take this."

He shrugged, "I have not been chosen for this quest, after all, and I have no use for it here. May it keep you safe."

"But..."

"Lily, you are my sister. If this is all I can do to protect you, please allow me to do it. You use a sword as well as I do...." His cheeks turned an odd color, and he looked down at his feet.

"Fine," Lily said. She traced the hilt Crocus held out to her with a long green finger. It had been enchanted to adjust to the grip of whoever held it.

As if on cue, it shrank to frog-size. She tested the weight and the balance of the blade, then tried a few strokes. Crocus was a talented weapon-maker. The sword felt like an extension of her arm. She sheathed Splinter and buckled it across her back over the cloak, feeling the added weight. "Thank you," she said, meeting her twin's eyes with her froggy orbs, "I'll take good care of it for you."

Crocus bobbed his head, looking sheepish. "You had better," he murmured, "and bring something back for me."

Lily tried to raise an eyebrow, but she didn't have those anymore. "We both know I can't draw."

Crocus shrugged. "Bring me back a rock or something then. I won't complain."

"We have one more present for you, my little froglet." Lily's mother held out a large satchel. Like the other items Lily had been given, it was enchanted to shrink to the size of the bearer when touched. Inside Ludwigia had placed the enchanted water flask, a sack of dried rations, a handful of stink spheres, some smoke tablets, and a few blue light tubes.

Lily hefted the satchel strap over her shoulder. She knew how each item should be used. "Thank you," she repeated, looking into the faces of her family.

The warmth of their love felt like an extra cloak around her shoulders and warmed her heart. They loved her. Supported her. Believed in her.

She felt a bubbly sensation in her stomach, a mix of excitement at the prospect of her journey, sadness that she was leaving, and guilt that she was going instead of Crocus. She was nervous at thought of stepping outside the swamp where she had lived her entire life, but she was ready for the adventure that awaited her.

"Time to go, my little froglet," her father scooped her into his hands. "We need to be at the edge of the mist before the sun gets much higher."

"Wait, Nelum." Ludwigia kissed the top of her daughter's tiny head. "We're so proud of you. We love you so much," she whispered, blinking away tears.

"Take down a dragon for me." Crocus attempted a smile as Lily was placed in a moss-lined basket for her journey to the edge of the swamp.

"She shouldn't be looking for dragons," Ludwigia scolded, as Nelum lifted the basket.

Lily tried to get one last look at the faces of her beloved family before the lid came down.

She heard her mother say, "Lily, find a nice safe prince to kiss." Then, she was enclosed in darkness.

* * *

In the basket, Lily kept her body flat and still, as the woven reeds under her feet were bounced and jolted.

At the edge of the forest, her basket was placed in the bed of a supply wagon. Over the years, Frogville had struck up a partnership with the merchants who passed through the town on their way to the city. In exchange for herbs and potions that could only be found in the swamp, the merchants transported the questors to the capital.

"Look for Prince Raymond," Nelum told his daughter. "He's known to be spoiled and a bit arrogant, but he sometimes grants favors in exchange for tasks."

"If I do his chores, I get a kiss?" Lily shuddered.

Nelum shrugged. "They usually don't ask for much. My great-great-uncle once had to retrieve a ball for one of the royal princesses. He was also given her hand in marriage, although she was a bit of a simpleton."

"Did he love her?" Lily's mind whirled, thinking of the strange figure. Had the stranger been wrong about the curse?

"Heavens no," Nelum chuckled. "He just wanted to get out of the swamp."

"Well, I have no intention of marrying Prince Raymond," Lily declared. "I'll get that kiss and come back home."

"Be careful, my little froglet."

"I will," Lily promised, as her father closed the basket lid again to protect her from the sun before the wagon began to roll. Her quest had begun.

CHAPTER 6

STRANDED

Lily's mid-morning nap was interrupted by shouts and curses. The wagon seemed to be going faster, hitting every bump and rock.

"Stop the wagon!" a distant shout echoed. "Pull over!"

Was this a robbery? Lily had heard of robberies. A boy named Thistle had told her that during his journey he'd observed a poor, weak man being beaten up by thieves who stole what little money he had. In his frog form, Thistle had been powerless to intervene, and the memory still caused him shame and anxiety.

"Pull over!"

The wagon hit another rut, and suddenly Lily was airborne. She winced and scrabbled as the basket crashed against the bed of the wooden wagon and rolled on its side. Another rut sent the basket bouncing even higher. Lily gasped in pain as she hit the wall of the woven container.

If she bounced higher, she thought she'd be thrown out of the wagon. Just then, she felt a third bounce and the basket flew into the air. After a long arc, it hit the ground. Lily winced, unable to control her movements. She tumbled around in her reed prison and was pelted by moss as the basket hit something hard, bounced once more, then rolled to a stop.

She lay in the jumble of damp moss, her breath caught in her throat. The sounds of horse hooves and carriage wheels faded into the distance, leaving an eerie silence. Bruised and sore, Lily kicked the lid off the basket and looked around.

A burning light from above nearly blinded her, making her pull the hood of her cloak down to shield her face. She looked around and saw golden hills in every direction without a trace of green. The air felt as hot as the forge in her father's weapons shop and her skin was drying out, even with the magic cloak her mother had given her.

She reached out an arm to touch the ground beneath her basket. It was hot and dry with a granular texture. She remembered the stories her father had told her and realized that she had landed in sand. *This must be the Sitis Desert, a place without water or any sort of moisture for miles,* she thought. She knew that in the desert her frog skin could dehydrate after a day or so, turning her a baked, leathery husk. For the first time, Lily felt a tingle of fear.

* * *

Night fell. Lily knew if she stayed in her basket, she'd die of thirst. She had to get out. The wagon wouldn't come back for her. The merchant must have long forgotten the little basket and its precious frog.

Guided by the stars, Lily started out across the sand toward the royal city. The sand stuck to her hands and feet as she hopped, but she kept going, following the wagon's tracks. She cracked open one of the glowing blue tubes to light her way.

At first, the night air had relieved the burning sun, but the temperature continued to drop and soon it was cold. She wrapped her cloak tighter around her body, trying to stay warm.

As a frog, she was even more susceptible to cold than other creatures were, and the colder it got, the more her body wanted to sleep, no matter how hard she fought to keep her eyes open. But she couldn't waste precious time. During the day, it would be too hot to travel, so she continued her trek across the sand, afraid that if she fell asleep in the desert, she'd never wake up.

She told herself that to stay alive, she'd have to stay awake; and, that she was a Frogville champion whose duty it was to succeed in her quest and return to her family. She repeated their names: Crocus, Mother, Father. Crocus, Mother, Father. Crocus, Mother, Father..." until she saw the first streaks of dawn on the horizon.

Soon the sun would be merciless; the sand would be scorching. She had to find shelter until nightfall, but no refuge was in sight. So, she burrowed deep into the sand until she reached the damp ground beneath it and used her web feet to wrap her cloak around her. Then she reached up to cover herself with a light layer of sand, so she would be hidden, protected from predators. The cool sand soothed her raw hands and feet and relieved her aching muscles. She was exhausted and within seconds she was asleep.

Lily dreamed that she was back on the island, but, except for the hills and trees, the swamp was unrecognizable. Instead of barren, grey land, the hills were covered with lush grass and flowers of every color. The surrounding waters were crystalline. The midday sun reflected on the surface and ripples lapped against the shore. Birds sang, swooping overhead, or gliding on the lake. Small animals drank from the water or ate the grass and shrubs that grew around the edges. The scene was quiet and peaceful, yet to Lily, it felt strange, unfamiliar.

"Beautiful, isn't it?" a voice said, and she turned to face the same figure from before, standing behind her. "Many years ago, your home was a very different place."

"But you cursed it," Lily replied. "Because we were selfish and greedy. Isn't that true?"

A chuckle flowed from the folds of the figure's cloak. "Oh, dear child, you think I am the wizard?" A knobby hand pushed back the hood of the cloak, revealing an ancient-looking woman. Her skin was pale and lined, and as thin and wrinkled as paper. A mane of pure white hair flowed over her shoulders. She smiled and her eyes twinkled.

"Do I look like a wizard?" she asked, her voice like honey.

"If you're not..." Lily frowned. "Then who are you?"

"My name is Asphodel," the old woman said, as she slowly lowered herself to the grass and patted a spot beside her. "I am the great-great-great-great-granddaughter of the wizard who cursed your village."

"If you're only his descendant," Lily said, hopping to sit beside her, "Why are you here instead of him?"

"Because in the last hundred years or so, he has fallen into a deep depression and given up hope of ever breaking the curse."

Lily sat patiently and waited, admiring the lapping water that stretched out before her.

"My-great-great-great-great-grandfather was always a bit of a fool," Asphodel admitted, twisting a blade of grass between her fingers. "He dreamed of becoming a great sorcerer but lacked the gift. He happened upon a magic book and practiced the spells without realizing the consequences, so he paid the price of his folly."

Lily stared at her in surprise.

"Oh yes, child. The spell he cast should not have had the effect it did, but he was playing with forces he didn't understand. No one will ever be free until you receive the kiss of true love."

"I won't fall in love with the prince," Lily stammered.

"We'll discuss that later, my child." Asphodel was twisting the grass blades into a bracelet. "I'm here to offer assistance if you like. I have reason to want the curse removed. I've lived for one hundred and ten years. This old body needs a rest."

Asphodel chuckled, then turned serious. "I am the last member of my family line. The last companion so to speak. I am the last one who is willing to help remove his curse. Once I am gone, the wizard will be alone." She looked at Lily, her eyes tired. "My time is growing short. My only wish is to release him from the spell."

"How can I receive a kiss of true love, when I'm trapped in the middle of a desert?" Lily demanded.

Asphodel smiled and tied the grass bracelet around Lily's wrist. "Don't lose this," she said. "I'll need to find you again."

"Can you help me get to the city?"

Asphodel shook her head and touched Lily's forehead. The gesture was light, but it seemed to push Lily back, away from the grass, the hill, and the lake.

"No need to worry. Help is on the way."

Lily heard the old woman's voice recede as the scene dissolved into darkness.

CHAPTER 7

A NEW ALLY

Lily awoke to the ground vibrating, and as the vibrations grew, she heard the sounds of wheels and hooves, of laughing and talking. And she smelled wood smoke.

She poked her head out of the sand and looked around. An entire camp, with tents of every size and color, had been erected around her hiding place, and strange, two-legged creatures scurried around carrying buckets of water and bundles of food.

Lily felt both relief and curiosity. Veteran travelers told tales of these people. So, these are outsiders, she thought, staring in wonder. They were all shapes and sizes. Their skin colors ranged from pasty white to pink, to tan, to dark brown. Some had more hair than others, with it either hanging down their backs or covering their cheeks and chins. Some wore long skirts that covered their legs and tripped them as they walked. Lily wondered if this was part of Asphodel's magic. Had she called these people here?

Lily needed water now, and the sound of splashing drew her attention. She watched one of the creatures dump grey water onto the sand, only a few yards away. She hopped as fast as she could toward a slender creature whose long, blond hair was woven into a braid. Some of the water had soaked into the ground, but some had been caught between rocks, creating puddles.

Lily splashed into a puddle, not caring that the water looked dirty or that food scraps floated in it. Her dry skin soaked up the water. The creature lifted another bucket and Lily could see that the water was cleaner. Without thinking, she spoke up.

"Excuse me, would you mind if I swam in that water before you dump it?"

The creature looked around in surprise, trying to locate the speaker.

"Down here," Lily called.

The creature's piercing blue eyes widened as it caught sight of Lily.

"Hi," Lily said and waved her little green arm.

The creature screamed and dropped the bucket

"Please. Please stop screaming." The shrill sound of the creature's voice was making Lily's head throb. "I won't hurt you."

The creature was silent. "Thank you," Lily said. "Might I jump into your bucket for a few minutes?"

The creature's face twisted with rage as it lifted its leg and swung it down so that Lily had to leap to avoid the heavy-looking shoe.

"Stop that!" Lily dodged the creature's foot again. "I'm harmless. I can't hurt you."

"Evil creature." The shoe came down again. "Disgusting, vile beast."

"Why must you be so rude?" Lily hopped again as the foot came down in a puddle, splashing dirty water everywhere. "I might have commented that you are a strange, short-legged creature with too-small eyes, but I was being polite."

Lily hopped onto the foot after it came down again and catapulted onto the creature's knee, then bounced off its hand and landed on its well-padded chest. The creature began to scream again.

Lily spat, shooting her long tongue into the creature's blue eye.

"Ugh!" the creature screamed so loudly that Lily put her hands over the places where her ears once were. The creature swatted at Lily, hurling her deep into the mud.

Lily pushed and kicked to free herself, while the creature laughed. "I've got you now." The creature smirked and lifted its foot for one more vicious stomp.

"Leave the poor thing alone." Lily saw a slim leg beneath ragged skirts.

"Get out of the way, Cassie, that thing's evil," the first creature snapped. "It talks and it poked me in the eye."

"It was defending itself, Susanna. What would you do if someone tried to step on you?"

"I step on things all the time. Nothing ever talks back to me."

"Well, maybe it's time something did!" Lily shouted.

"Did you hear that? It's an evil creature."

"I am not evil," Lily said, "I'm enchanted, while you, whatever you may be, are just ugly and mean."

Cassie looked down at Lily, whose eyes glowed gold. "Maybe you shouldn't talk so much while I'm trying to save you," she said before turning back to Susanna. "Why don't I handle this, and you go take my place in the dining room? Prince Raymond has a big appetite tonight."

"Really?" Susanna's voice rose in excitement. "Fine. But if this *thing* causes any trouble, I'll tell Wilfred it's your fault." With that, she dashed off, holding her skirts above her ankles.

"You poor thing, are you okay?" When Cassie crouched to dig her out of the mud, Lily had a chance to take a good look at her protector. Cassie's skin was a rich golden brown, like the coppery mud that surrounded them. Her eyes were almond-shaped, gold, with flecks of green. Her nose was too large and her mouth too small to be beautiful by Frogville standards, but when she smiled, Lily was surprised that she didn't seem as ugly as the other creatures.

"You poor thing," Cassie said again, as she gently lifted Lily and held her in her hands. "You almost got squashed a few times."

"Thanks to you, I didn't." Lily realized that she was covered in mud and eyed the last bucket of water. "If I promise to be on my way and not cause any more trouble, will you kindly allow me to soak in that water bucket? I'm very thirsty."

Cassie's warm chuckle was pleasing to Lily's ears. "I'll get you some clean water instead. That way you can wash and drink, as well."

Cassie carried Lily to a patched tent, where she helped her wash the mud from her cloak, then filled a small bowl with clean water. Lily removed the cloak, pouch, and sword from her shoulders and all three enchanted items returned to their original sizes.

Cassie's eyes widened. "Are you a magic frog?"

Lily hopped into the bowl, making sure her sword was within reach. "Not magic, but enchanted. There's a difference."

"Really?" Cassie propped her chin in her hands. "Do tell."

Lily told her about Frogville's curse, how every boy was trained for the quest, and how she'd expected to stay behind while her brother went on his adventure but had been given the responsibility and burden instead.

"Hmmm. You can't just get a kiss from anyone?" Cassie asked.

"Tradition dictates that it must be someone of royal blood," Lily explained. "Though Asphodel told me that a kiss of true love would free the whole town."

"Well, you're in luck, sort of," Cassie said. "I'm a servant with Prince Raymond's traveling party. At this moment, you are very close to someone of royal blood. But…" her face twisted into a frown, "It seems he is only able to love himself."

Lily's heart skipped. "I'm close to someone of royal blood?"

Cassie nodded. "His Highness follows his own tradition. He must save a damsel in distress before his eighteenth birthday. He is going to save a princess who is held captive by a dragon on the other side of the desert." She rolled her eyes. "Prince Raymond brought half the servants in the castle with him to be sure he'd be properly dressed, bathed, and fed during his quest. He won't even walk if he can ride in a cushioned sedan chair."

A sound outside the door made Cassie flinch. "Be sure he doesn't hear you repeat that," she added in a quieter voice. "He's not very forgiving."

"Will you help me meet him?" Lily asked. "If I explain my situation, maybe he'll be willing to help."

Cassie shook her head. "That's not a good idea."

"Why not?"

"He hates things that are… sorry… dirty." Cassie cocked her head and frowned.

Lily looked at her small, bumpy, green body. She wasn't dirty, was she?

"And Prince Raymond never does anything he's not paid to do."

Lily's spirits sank. She'd come so close to receiving a royal kiss and failed. What could she do now? Even if she knew where to find another prince, she wouldn't survive crossing the desert. She had to find a way to meet Prince Raymond and obtain his kiss, even if it wasn't a kiss of true love.

Cassie was making a small bed of damp rags for her, but Lily wasn't ready to sleep yet. She had to try again. "Would you be willing to help me find the prince? No one would have to know. You could just show me which tent is his."

Apprehension flashed across Cassie's caramel-colored features, then they melted into a smile. "If he sees you, he will surely order someone to stomp on you."

Lily hopped out of the bowl and reached for her cloak, swirling it over her shoulders as it shrank. She strapped on her pouch and settled Splinter in place, feeling the solid, comforting weight of her brother's weapon.

"If you help me find the prince, I will find a way to make him speak with me." Lily hoped she sounded more confident than she felt.

CHAPTER 8

MEET PRINCE RAYMOND

Raymond was the most handsome — and the most infamous — prince in the kingdom. He was tall, with rippling muscles, not a hint of fat, and a face so exquisite it might have been sculpted in marble. His eyes were as blue as the summer sky. His golden hair was always coiffed in a perfect peak. The sight of him left women weak in the knees, but in Lily's eyes, he was the ugliest creature in the world.

His eyes were too small. His nose too big. Lily noticed that he ate with all the finesse of a starving vulture.

From her vantage point in Cassie's pocket, she watched him consume several turkey legs, half a loaf of bread, and several goblets of wine. He chewed with his mouth open, so that his companions had to look at the mashed-up food and saliva between his teeth. He sampled from every plate placed before him and cast aside those that displeased him.

"Why does he waste so much food?" Lily asked Cassie, as the prince took a single bite of mushroom pastie, then threw it on the ground.

"He's royalty," Cassie whispered. "He can do as he likes."

"He's permitted to throw away all this food?"

"The servants who have won his favor are given the uneaten dishes," Cassie replied as she loaded the rejected plates on a cart. "The rest of us do our best to steal the scraps."

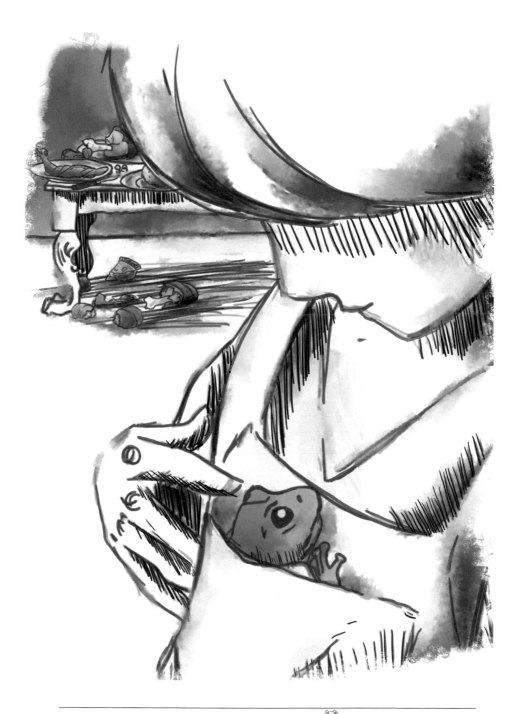

To illustrate her point, she slipped half a quiche into her pocket for Lily. It was enormous, but Lily ate it with gusto. She hadn't had a proper meal in two days.

"Given how much food he eats, I'm surprised Prince Raymond isn't fat," Lily said.

"He's very proud of his figure. He exercises constantly." Cassie pointed to a short, dumpling shaped man at Prince Raymond's side. "It's rumored that he is terrified of looking like his half-brother there, Prince Sebastian the Turgid. His aide Wilfred records the amount of food he eats each day, as well as the amount of exercise he does."

Across the room, Prince Raymond emptied another goblet of wine, then belched.

Lily was appalled. "He cares only for eating and exercising to remain slim? Has he no concern for ruling the kingdom? Has he no care for his people?"

Cassie leaned down and spoke softly so that the other servants wouldn't hear her. "His father, King Stephan, had many wives and many children. Prince Raymond is a long way from the throne."

"Then why must he slay a dragon and rescue a princess?"

Cassie shrugged. "Tradition."

"I will certainly never fall in love with him," Lily declared, as she watched Prince Raymond check his teeth in the reflection of a silver tray for bits of food. "But I can still try to get a kiss."

"Prince Raymond is not the sort of person who gives away favors," Cassie said. "Remember, he doesn't like... dirty things."

"I'm willing to take the risk," Lily said. "Excuse me." With that, she leaped from Cassie's pocket onto the table and raced toward the prince.

At first, no one noticed the little frog hopping over plates as she threaded her way around bowls and serving platters. But when she vaulted over a half-eaten turkey, one of the serving maids noticed her, let out a shriek, and dropped a tray of quail eggs, which crashed to the ground.

"Eew! Frog!" she screamed, pointing to Lily. The other servers scattered, bumping into tables as they ran out of the tent, while the few who remained tried to catch Lily.

Lily dodged left, grabbed a handful of jelly from a bowl, and threw it in her attacker's eye, then somersaulted over a jug of milk and landed on the handle of a ladle filled with gravy. Her weight was enough to splash a manservant when he reached for the little frog, who dove between his grasping fingers while he mopped his eyes with the other hand.

Servants on either side of the table blocked her approach to the prince, but just as they lunged toward her, she used her strong back legs to leap into the air and perform a graceful backflip over a roasted pig, landing on Prince Raymond's plate.

"Your Highness," Lily said, bowing low. "I wish to beg a favor." Prince Raymond held a carving knife in one hand.

"Do you dare to assassinate me, frog?" His sky-blue eyes were flashing.

Lily raised her hands in surrender. The man was many times her size. Reaching for her trusty sword, Splinter, would be futile. "You have nothing to fear," she said, in her loudest, most confident voice. "I am a citizen of Frogville. I mean no harm."

"You have interrupted my meal and disturbed my staff!"

"Most of your staff deserted you in a cowardly manner. And those who remained were easily hindered by the food they served you," Lily replied. "I acted in self-defense so that I could reach you, Your Highness."

"Aha. So, you admit I was your target." Prince Raymond looked triumphant.

"You imply that I wished to harm you, sir. I merely wished to humbly beseech you to grant me a small favor."

Prince Raymond still held the carving knife menacingly above Lily's head.

"Why should I grant you a favor?" he asked, wrinkling his nose in disgust.

Wilfred, the prince's aide, who had been hiding behind his magisterial chair, stepped out. He was a short man with a paunchy belly, thinning brown hair, and nervous blue eyes.

"If I may, Your Highness," he said," your family has had many interactions with Frogville, and while they are a small, secluded town, your mother regards them as unofficial allies of the crown since they provide the castle with scented candles."

Prince Raymond eyed Lily. "Why would my mother befriend frogs?"

"Forgive my appearance, Your Highness." Lily tried to disguise her exasperation. This prince was as dull as Burhead. "I'm under a spell that has transformed my person."

Prince Raymond looked at Lily, then Wilfred. "Am I to believe that a spell has turned you into a frog?"

No, you fool, I'm a chicken, Lily thought, but she held her tongue. "Yes, Your Highness, that is exactly what has happened."

Prince Raymond stroked his chin. "And you wish me to grant you a favor. What is it?"

"If I am to break the spell, I must be kissed by someone of royal blood," she explained in a rush. "If you would be willing to grant me…"

But Prince Raymond had already pushed himself back from the table with a look of revulsion.

"Absolutely not," he said, pinching his nose. "The very idea is abhorrent."

Nor am I eager to kiss your ugly face, Lily thought but she tried her best to remain calm. This was her only chance, and she couldn't afford to waste it.

"I beg of you, Your Highness. I have no hope of finding a man of such noble lineage as yours."

Prince Raymond shuddered as he strode toward the entrance to his tent. "It is no concern of mine whether you break your curse or not."

Lily hopped along the table after him. "But only you can help me," she pleaded. "Where shall I find another prince?"

"Try the royal city," Prince Raymond snapped. "You'll find plenty of us there."

"But Your Highness. I am no more than a little frog who will surely die in the desert."

"Again, no concern of mine." Prince Raymond had reached the entrance and Wilfred hastened to open the tent flap for him. "Good luck to you."

Lily's heart thudded. She couldn't fail now. She was so close. "If you help me, I will do anything you ask," she shouted at the top of her tiny frog lungs.

Prince Raymond paused one polished boot already out of the tent. He turned toward Lily.

"Anything?"

Lily nodded.

"And how good is your word?"

"I have never broken a promise, Your Highness."

The prince looked skeptical. "Let us be clear. If you do as I ask, I will help you lift your... curse." His lip curled with disgust.

Lily nodded, hope warming her heart. "Yes, sir."

"But first," Prince Raymond stroked his chin again. "I will test you to see how capable you truly are."

CHAPTER 9

FIVE AGAINST ONE

"These five men are my best soldiers," Prince Raymond gestured toward the men scattered around the small tent. From her place in Cassie's hand, Lily could see a swordsman standing in each corner of the enclosure and one standing near a pedestal in the center. "Every one of them is a highly-trained archer and swordsman, dedicated to protecting my royal person."

"You need five people to keep you safe?" Lily asked. She remembered that Prince Raymond was far from first in line to the throne.

"His Highness is a very important person who must be kept safe," Wilfred huffed.

"Oh." Lily turned her attention to the assembled men and waved, "Hi."

The soldiers responding by pulling their swords from their sheaths and arranging themselves in a ready stance.

"Do you see the necklace my soldier is guarding on the pedestal?"

Lily saw a large gold chain with a diamond pendant the size of her head lying on a velvet cushion. "Yes, sir."

"Bring that to me and you will have passed my test."

"And you will help me remove my curse?"

"Hmph. We shall see."

"Your Highness," Cassie bowed her head, "forgive me, but

considering Lily's size and the expertise of your men, is this test, perhaps too difficult?"

"How dare you question His Highness?" Wilfred roared.

Cassie shrank from his gaze.

The prince raised his hand. "Enough, Wilfred." He pointed to Lily. "This creature has come to me with an absurd request. If I must grant such an unpleasant favor, the creature must grant me an unequally unpleasant one. Unless it wishes to try its luck with another prince, these are my conditions."

Cassie's cheeks flushed pink.

Before she could irk the prince further, Lily hopped around to face her. "If this task is necessary to break my curse," she said. "I will do it."

"Excellent." Prince Raymond turned on his heels. "Come, Wilfred."

He swept out of the tent with Wilfred scuttling at his heels.

Cassie reluctantly followed behind them. "Good luck," she whispered and gently set Lily on the ground.

Lily felt a renewed sense of joy. She'd only known Cassie for a few hours, but this beautiful girl had risked her life by speaking up on her behalf.

"Thank you," she whispered.

Cassie gave her a faint smile and hurried off.

As the tent flap closed, Lily eyed the five men. Her only hope of surviving was to leap onto the pedestal and snatch the pendant before they could oppose her. She took a deep breath. One frog against five highly trained, heavily armed men.

The tent was small and cramped. She would have to be careful. A single swing from any of their swords would mean death. Then she scrutinized the situation with fresh eyes. The men were wearing bulky armor, which would weigh them down and prevent them from moving nimbly. And because the tent was small and the soldiers' speed hindered, an errant swing could do more damage to the other men than to her.

Her lithe little body was designed for escape. A smile bloomed on her lips. While the soldiers were large and sluggish, she was small and fast. She held the advantage.

Lily slipped a hand inside her pouch and found a round object. Why not raise the stakes for the men and make it even more difficult for them to attack? She bent her knees and leaped towards the closest swordsman. As she expected, his heavy armor made it difficult for him to react.

She used her powerful legs to launch herself from his boot and soar through the air to the flat of his sword blade, then shoot ten feet higher. Her head thumped the roof of the tent then, when she saw all the men looking in her direction, she threw the object she'd dug out of her pouch. The smoke tablet expanded to its natural size as it left her hand, and cracked when it hit the ground, releasing a thick cloud.

Panic broke out among the soldiers as the smoke obscured their vision. They were blinded and didn't dare swing their swords for fear of injuring their comrades. They blundered around, shouting and cursing, trying to find the tent flap to so they could open it to get rid of the smoke.

Lily was back on the ground, easily dodging their heavy boots as she made her way towards the pedestal. The fifth soldier remained at his post, one hand on the diamond necklace, but his eyes were so red and swollen from the smoke that he was unable to see.

She knew that if she tried to snatch the pendant, he'd try to squash her. She had to make him remove his hand, force him to focus on something else. She touched Splinter, which was still strapped to her back. If she cut the soldier with her sword, he'd let go of the necklace long enough for her to grab it. But the idea of injuring a man for following orders bothered her. She released her hold on Splinter's hand-grip. She'd use her weapon if absolutely necessary, but she saw there was another option.

Lily dug her hand into her pouch again, this time retrieving a stink sphere. The smell was atrocious but harmless. She threw the sphere on the ground, releasing the horrible stench. The man immediately withdrew his hold on the pendant to grab his nose. In that instant, she leaped to the pedestal, snatched the pendant, and fled, dragging the heavy gold chain behind her. She struggled to carry it on her back, staggering and dodging soldiers who were blinded by the smoke and overwhelmed by the putrid odor. The tent flap was just ahead. A few more hops and she would be free. She'd almost reached the flap when it billowed open and Prince Raymond stepped inside.

He backed away from the horrendous smell and the choking haze. His face turned red as he struggled to breathe.

"Merciful heavens," he sputtered. "What happened here?"

One of the soldiers wheezed, "That lousy frog is magic indeed, sir. It cast a spell to create smoke and another to release this horrid stench."

"I did no such thing..." Lily protested. At that moment, Cassie re-entered the tent and scooped her up. All eyes turned to her. She realized that revealing her limited stash of weapons wouldn't be the best strategy. If she fooled him into thinking she was more powerful than she really was, the prince would be more likely to kiss her out of fear for what she might do next.

"Three spells," Lily fibbed. "One for the smoke. One for the stench," she eyed the five soldiers, "and a third that will cause your fingers and toes to fall off if any of you attack me again."

Prince Raymond glared at her. He would have preferred to throw her back in the tent to face the soldiers than admit she'd passed the test. But if she was telling the truth, his men would lose their fingers and toes, making them useless.

"You cheated," he hissed.

Lily smiled, "On the contrary, Your Highness. You ordered me to take the pendant from the pedestal. You did not specify how it must be accomplished."

"Because I didn't think you could do it!" Prince Raymond scowled. "Very well," he said through gritted teeth, "I will grant your favor."

Relief coursed through Lily's body. "Thank you, sir."

"But first," the price tapped a finger on his lips, "I demand another task, another favor, if you will."

Lily looked at the five soldiers, all still green around the gills. "Will you put me in a tent with ten men now?"

"No, you silly creature." The prince straightened his shoulders. "That was just a test. Now I require a real challenge."

"Fine," Lily sighed. She had come this far. What was another close call with death?

Prince Raymond's smile was menacing. "You will go to the dragon's den, steal his strength-giving amulet, and bring it to me."

CHAPTER 10

IMPORTANT INFORMATION

prince Raymond sprawled across the long bench in his velvet-lined carriage as the traveling party made its way to the dragon's cavern. Outside the curtained window, the sun blazed. Through a small opening, Lily could see sweat pouring from the driver's brow as he urged the horses forward. Cassie and Wilfred waved hand fans to keep Prince Raymond cool, while Lily swam in a shallow bowl of water.

"The dragon, Ignis, is a ferocious monster, but without his amulet, he is as docile as a kitten. Which is why he keeps it hidden. No knight has ever been able to reach it."

"Does everyone know that his amulet is his source of strength?" Lily asked.

"Of course not," Wilfred sniffed, his face glistening with sweat. He ignored his own discomfort while devotedly fanning the prince. "The kingdom's top scholars obtained this information. A great deal of time has been spent searching for a quest suitable for His Highness, one that would not…"

"Wouldn't get him killed?" Lily asked.

"Tradition doesn't require the prince to die in the pursuit," Wilfred said.

"Quiet!" Prince Raymond snapped. He glowered at Lily. "I have commanded you to perform a favor for me, which in no way implies that I am a coward."

"Your Highness, I would never imply anything of the kind."

Lily's voice dripped with sarcasm. "You have simply ordered a little frog to steal an object so that you can easily defeat a ferocious dragon."

Prince Raymond's ears turned red. "One more word and I will have you thrown from the carriage,"

"My apologies," Lily said, then muttered to herself, "You lazy, cowardly, spoiled brat."

"If you will pardon my boldness, Your Highness," Cassie said quietly. "I beg you to describe the amulet. Lily will need to identify it properly."

Prince Raymond scowled again. "Wilfred, show them the drawing."

Wilfred stopped fanning long enough to pull a scrap of parchment from his pocket. "As you can see, the amulet is a square-cut topaz of reddish-hue set on a gold chain." He resumed fanning the prince with his free hand. "Our scholars discovered a footnote in an ancient document that mentions a spell to protect the power within."

"If the amulet is the source of his strength, he will do everything in his power to protect it," Lily said.

Cassie looked worried. "Did the footnote mention what the spell does? Will Lily be hurt as she carries it away?"

Wilfred shrugged, "The scholar's research failed to specify what the spell would do."

"What does it matter to you? You are not risking your life to steal it." Cassie retorted.

"One more word and I will have you thrown from the carriage with the frog," the prince threatened.

"I have a name, sir," Lily said. "It is Lilypad Lotus Dillweed."

Prince Raymond raised an eyebrow. "Of course, it is. Your amusing name does not interest me. My only concern is that you manage to enter the dragon's cave and retrieve the amulet so that I can rescue the princess."

Lily's anger rose. How dare the pompous prince speak to her and Cassie that way? She needed his kiss to break her curse, but she wouldn't allow him to bully her. Then a new thought came to mind, and she felt calm drifting over her.

She smiled up at the prince. "No," she said.

"No? May I remind you that I am the key to removing your wretched curse? Or would you prefer to try your luck finding someone else of royal blood in the desert?"

"You are not going to throw me or my friend out of this carriage, because I am the key to your success, Your Highness." Lily puffed out her chest, a bold stance for a frog. "You are not willing to risk your life to save the princess, and I have observed that none of your soldiers is loyal enough to risk his life to save you. You need me." Lily took the prince's silence as a sign of agreement.

"And since that is true," she said, "I will require a few things from you. First, you must not threaten me or my friend or suggest that you might withhold your part of this bargain by refusing to kiss me. You will treat me and my friend, Cassie, with respect. She will eat real food, not your scraps, and she will receive better wages."

"She is not paid wages," Wilfred protested.

"Much. Better. Wages." Lily said.

"But. But…" Wilfred sputtered.

"Wilfred, be quiet." The prince studied Lily for a moment, then continued, "If I agree to your demands, what will you give me in return?"

"I will retrieve the amulet from the dragon's cavern and bring it to you."

Prince Raymond's eyes narrowed, "You have already agreed to do that."

Lily smiled, "Yes, sir. I am only pointing out that we are on equal footing. If I fail to receive a royal kiss, I will remain a frog."

The prince nodded.

"But, if I risk my life in the dragon's cave and you refuse to kiss me, I will not be obliged to give you the amulet. You will be unable to rescue the princess and will return to your father—a failure."

The prince flinched.

"Sir," Wilfred blustered, "you are not obligated."

"Silence, Wilfred!"

For a moment, Lily saw a faint light of respect in the prince's eyes.

"You are holding my quest over my head. Clever, Miss… Dillweed."

Lily lifted her chin. "Yes, Your Highness."

The prince nodded. "Very well. I concede defeat. What more do you wish to know about your mission?"

"Are we sure that the princess is being held in the cave?" She didn't want to anger a dragon for no reason.

"Of that, we are quite sure," Wilfred said. He pulled another piece of parchment from his pocket and showed Lily a portrait of a striking young woman with flowing red tresses and violet eyes. "Princess Belinda is the sixth daughter of King James, monarch of the Province of Lamia. She is said to be the most beautiful among her sisters. Many suitors wished to marry her before she was kidnapped by the dragon. The king has promised her rescuer her hand in marriage, along with a sizable dowry."

Lily thought hard, reviewing her history lessons for mention of the province of Lamia. "What is this kingdom known for?"

Prince Raymond shrugged, unconcerned.

Wilfred frowned. "Not much is known about the kingdom. It is thought to be a small but wealthy province."

"And you are not sure how their wealth is earned?"

Prince Raymond shrugged again. "What does it matter? My mission is to rescue the princess. Yours is to steal the amulet. The source of the family wealth is irrelevant."

Lily knew he was right, but something about the mystery bothered her.

"Sir," Wilfred said, "we are fast approaching our campsite."

Outside the window, Lily saw a wide expanse of white, which she realized must be salt. Long ago, her father had told her that the desert of Sitis had once been an ocean. Now only lumps of white, hardened sea salt remained. A memory tugged at her. During one of the classes she'd taken with Crocus, Master Hopsley had mentioned that someone used salt for something. She turned to Wilfred. "Is there a body of water near the dragon's cave?"

The aide raised his eyebrows. "How did you know that? In fact, there is. It's an oasis for the dragon's guards."

"If you're planning to swim into the cave, you're out of luck." Prince Raymond scoffed. "The cave is separated from the pool of water by a stretch of land."

"Not what I needed the water for at all, Your Highness." Lily splashed in the bowl in circles. "Might your cooking staff have a few kettles I can borrow?"

***

The prince's carriage stopped a distance from the dragon's cave. His elite squadron of soldiers pulled their carriages to a stop nearby. They assembled under the trees while Lily explained her idea to the prince and his troops. Once he understood the plan of attack, the prince sent a few of his men to the supply wagon to collect pots, while others were dispatched to the salt flats to gather chunks of it.

Under the cover of darkness, they carried the salt and pots to the forest, where they would guard them until sunrise. Lily and Cassie went to the kitchen wagon to gather the necessary supplies for extra potions.

Sleeping tents were set up to keep everyone safe from the chill night air. When Prince Raymond went to his tent to be fed and prepare for a good night's sleep, Lily and Cassie retired to their own tent to prepare potions.

"Does it seem unfair to you that we're working while the prince sleeps?" Lily asked, as she added another stink sphere to the neat line of them along the side of the tent.

Cassie shrugged, "I have been in the royal family's service all my life." She placed her somewhat misshapen stink sphere with the others. "He has always slept while those around him worked."

"Does the rest of your family work for the royal family, too?" Lily asked.

Cassie was silent for a moment. "I never knew my family. The palace cook found me in a wine cask by the kitchen door. I was named Cassie, which sounds like the word 'cask,' but a little nicer." She began to mix the potion for another stink sphere. "The cook assumed that my parents must have been too poor to feed me, so they left me in the hope I'd be adopted."

"Do you wish you could live a different kind of life?"

Cassie snickered, "Of course. But where would I go? What would I do? I have no money, and I have no other skill than serving the royal family."

Lily's damp hand patted Cassie's. "If I survive the dragon, you can return to Frogville with me. My mother and father sell potions, and my brother..." Lily hesitated. She wondered if her twin brother was still sad. Perhaps he was relieved that he had been spared this quest. Was he happy to be helping their mother in her shop? She had no doubt Crocus was still the same person he had always been, a kind, patient force in the face of all obstacles. She also had no doubt he would welcome the girl who helped his sister successfully complete her quest. "They would love to meet you, Cassie," she said.

Cassie's brows furrowed. "Lily, do you believe you will succeed in retrieving the amulet?"

Lily paused before beginning a new stink sphere. "I must. If I want to be free, I must."

That night Lily dreamed of Asphodel. She saw the old woman seated at a table in what looked like a stone tower.

The walls were covered with the scrawling of a madman hundreds of equations and notations. Some appeared to be more recent than others. Some were smudged and lichen grew over them, as though they had been there for many years.

Asphodel was scribbling notes on a scrap of paper, but she looked up when she noticed Lily in the room.

"What are you doing?" she demanded, pushing herself up from the table. "I told you how to break the enchantment for good. Now you're risking your life for a kiss that will only free you?" She winced and put a hand to her chest. "I'm running out of time."

"Have you seen the prince?" Lily retorted. "He is the most arrogant, self-absorbed egomaniac I have ever met. I'm sorry that I can't free everyone from the spell, but I refuse to love him. I'll have to go back to my village and tell the next quester how to break the spell forever."

"You haven't been listening to me," Asphodel's eyes flashed with anger. "I told you, true love's kiss…"

They heard a crash outside the room, the sound of glass shattering as if something had been thrown in a fit of anger.

Then a roar of fury echoed through the tower.

Lily felt the dream slipping away.

Asphodel moved stiffly towards the door. "I must leave you. The wizard is having a temper tantrum again. You must remember, true love is the only way."

A snore woke Lily from her dream. She looked around the tent, trying to remember where she was, then spied the extra stink spheres and smoke tablets lined along one side of the tent. Cassie was snoring softly, wrapped in a jumble of blankets. Her tangled mass of curls formed a halo around her face.

Lily jumped as Cassie snorted again, stretched like a cat, and rolled onto her side. The snoring decreased and Lily felt warmth spread through her veins. She'd only known Cassie for two days, but she felt as though she'd known her all her life. She was kind, generous, loyal to a fault, with surprising and charming facets of her personality popping out when least expected. Lily wanted to bring her home so they could be friends forever.

At the sound of another roar, Lily hopped out of her bowl of water to peer through the tent flap. Dawn was breaking. Pale, silvery light crept over the horizon. Lily searched the clouds for the form of a dragon about to attack the camp, but the sky was clear.

She shook her head and started packing her potions and weapons in her pouch. Why should she worry that the dragon might find them when she was about to attack him?

CHAPTER 11

PLAN OF ATTACK

Decked in a suit of armor, Prince Raymond stood atop a platform built of elder wood and trimmed in gold leaf. As he addressed the soldiers, his golden chest plate reflected his flaxen hair.

"Our plan is simple." He tossed an indigo cape over his shoulder.

"*Our* plan?" Cassie chuckled. "Does he realize that he's taking the credit for your idea?"

"It wasn't easy to make him to understand the plan when I explained it to him," Lily giggled.

Cassie cupped her hands and raised Lily over her head. "I'll hold you up so everyone can see you."

"That's sweet." Lily patted her friend's thumb. "But it's better for the soldiers to believe that their orders come from the prince."

"We'll distract the dragon." The prince said, pointing in the direction of the cavern.

A rumble of voices arose. "We are ready, Your Highness."

"Uh, for a few..." he glanced in Lily's direction, then continued. "That will allow a few stealth troops to enter the cavern."

He raised his voice taking command of the crowd. "Once the stealth troops are inside, we will make a fast, calculated retreat through the forest." The prince scanned the faces of his men. "I don't want to hear any talk of noble self-sacrifice. Our mission is to get our operatives into the cavern, then we will wait until nightfall for the signal."

"Do you have what you need to send the signal?" Cassie whispered.

Lily patted her pouch. "When I pull the string at the bottom of the device, colored light will soar through the air."

"Be careful not to set it off by accident," Cassie murmured. "I'll be watching the sky until I know you're safe."

"Don't fret." Lily patted Cassie's hand. "I'll hop in and out of there so fast you won't even miss me."

Cassie looked Lily in the eye. "If you're inside too long, I'll come after you."

"You'll do nothing of the sort," Lily said. "That would only make my task more difficult. Then I'd have to retrieve the amulet and protect you, too."

"I'm not a helpless princess," Cassie protested. "I won't need to be rescued."

"Helpless or not, you can't hide under a small rock from the dragon. I can."

"Ahem. Excuse me." Wilfred was standing in front of them. "The soldiers are heading out," he sniffed, his mouth set in a thin line. "It's time for us to leave." He held out a tray.

"Right." Lily hopped onto the tray he was holding, then changed her mind and hopped back into Cassie's hand. "I meant it when I asked you to return to Frogville with me—assuming I survive the dragon."

Cassie gave her a thin, worried smile. "I look forward to seeing you soon then. I'd love to meet your family."

Lily hopped back to Wilfred's tray. "You will. I promise."

When Lily and Wilfred arrived, Prince Raymond was supervising five groups of soldiers. Each group was equipped with a kettle filled with salt blocks, which were melting over small fires.

"We might as well be waving a banner announcing that we're here," the prince said when he saw Wilfred and Lily.

"The plan will work," Lily assured him, trying to sound more confident than she felt. She had prepared a handful of smoke tablets and stink spheres for each of the five groups and asked Wilfred to be sure they were distributed. "

Prince Raymond motioned to a trio of men standing apart near a longer catapult meant for distance. "These are my best marksmen," he said. "They can hit the eye of a gnat flying a hundred yards away."

"Really?" Lily was surprised. In the two days she'd known the prince, he'd never been inclined to bestow praise on anyone.

"They are my best men," he repeated.

She nodded, accepting his assertion as fact. "All right then." She surveyed the men. "Aim carefully, please. I'd like to land just outside the entrance to the cavern without hitting the wall."

The three men looked to Prince Raymond for confirmation. He nodded. "Do as Miss Dillweed asks."

Wilfred passed Lily off to one of the three marksmen who took his place in the catapult line. "Sir," he said, "I have inspected the kettles. The salt has melted. Any longer and it will burn."

Prince Raymond looked at Lily, who hopped onto the catapult. She nodded.

He addressed the soldiers. "Right to left, you will fire every five seconds."

"Yes, sir." The men responded as one.

"Very good." The prince pointed to the first of the five groups. "Fire!" The men released the catapult loaded with a kettle of molten salt, which exploded when it hit the freezing lake.

A fifty-foot column of water shot into the air with a sonic bang, followed five seconds later by another bang as a second kettle was released, and then a third. This was the diversion Lily had planned. It would focus the dragon away from her as she entered his cavern.

A glimmer of red appeared at the mouth of the cavern, and Lily knew that Ignis was watching the show.

"Now!" she commanded the soldiers manning her catapult. As the fourth kettle shot into the lake, they released her. The column of water was a perfect cover as she soared through the air, heading straight for the mouth of the dragon's cavern. As she hit the peak of her flight, she shook out her cloak, and the ends billowed like a sail. She clung to the straps Cassie had sewn into the sides. They turned the cloak into a parachute that caught the wind and floated her down to earth as gently as a dandelion's seed head.

Just as the last kettle hit the lake, the dragon rushed out of his cavern and looked up. With exquisite timing, Lily floated ten feet over his head before landing. He bolted for the lake without noticing her.

The forest was enveloped in fog, which hid the prince's soldiers. Lily knew the dragon would be unable to see them.

At her instruction, the prince had ordered each of his men to crush a smoke tablet and release a stink sphere the moment Ignis was spotted flying toward the trees. Then they would all rush back to their camp.

The stench of rotten eggs wafting over the water assured her that the stink spheres had been broken. She smiled in triumph as she touched the ground. The plan was working. The smoke would hide the men as they retreated into the trees, while the putrid odor would hide their scent from the dragon. If they laid low, Prince Raymond and his soldiers would be safe from Ignis until she found the amulet.

Lily slipped into the cavern, staying close to the shadows of the walls. The light from the entrance revealed several tunnels leading in different directions. Unsure of which to take, she slipped behind a stalagmite and waited. Minutes later, she heard the leathery beat of wings as Ignis re-entered the cave, bringing with him the slight scent of smoke and sulfur. She had planned to silently follow the dragon until he led her to the amulet.

"Ignis?" She heard a rustle of silk and slippered feet on the stone floor. "What was all the commotion?"

"I don't know, princess," the dragon rumbled. "I saw no trace in the water, but several cooking pots floated on the surface."

"What is that horrid odor?" the princess asked. "What was that in the trees?"

"The forest is covered with a cloud of smoke. With your permission, I will search for an encampment."

Permission? Lily caught a glimpse of the princess. Why would the dragon need his captive's permission?

"No, stay here." The princess tossed a lock of flame-colored hair over her shoulder. "Doubtless a prince was making a commotion to draw you from this cavern."

Lily waited for one of them to speak again.

The princess laughed, "I'd prefer to keep you here to be certain of a good fight. The suitors must be made to prove themselves."

"As you wish, princess," Ignis bowed his head.

Something was very wrong. The back of Lily's neck prickled with unease. She hopped a little closer, trying to get a better look at the princess.

Princess Belinda examined her nails. "It's tiresome to wait in this drafty cavern." She walked into a pool of light and Lily caught sight of something glinting on her chest, the square-cut topaz of reddish hue on a golden chain.

Lily swallowed a gasp. The amulet allowed her to control the dragon, who was powerless without it. Princess Belinda wasn't the helpless captive Prince Raymond assumed she was.

"I'm looking forward to this fight, but you must not forget to lose." Her voice echoed off the walls. "I will marry any dolt who shows up, then overtake his throne."

Lily ducked back into the shadows. Not only was the princess evil and controlling, but she was also scheming to take over Prince Raymond's kingdom.

She decided to get out and warn the prince before it was too late.

CHAPTER 12

A TRAP?

As the sun set, the shadows lengthened, and the light faded until the cavern was shrouded in darkness. Lily waited for Princess Belinda to retire for the night before she came out of hiding and stretched her legs.

Ignis the Dragon was sound asleep, and his snoring vibrated like the rumble of far-off thunder. Lily's first thought had been to escape as soon as night fell and warn Prince Raymond. But if she did that, Princess Belinda would still possess the dragon's power, and would no doubt use it to conquer the kingdom of any prince who tried to rescue her. So, Lily decided to steal the amulet before warning Prince Raymond of the princess's true nature.

Easier said than done, she thought, as she slipped out of her corner and hopped down the tunnel that led to the Princess's chamber. She thought she might need a glow tube to light the way, but her new frog eyes could see surprisingly well in the darkness. She was amazed at the princess's bedroom, which resembled her mother's potion shop, filled with bottles, beakers of variously colored liquids, and books that all seemed to be about magic.

She wondered if the princess planned to use these potions to take over a kingdom and felt a grudging respect for her. She didn't approve of Princess Belinda's thirst for power and treachery, but she was impressed at the signs of her craft. This princess was no damsel in distress. It would've been easier if she had been.

Lily spotted the princess fast asleep on a high, canopied

bed. She looked almost angelic, her red locks streaming around her as she lay on the silk sheets, surrounded by mountains of pillows. But there was nothing angelic about her. The princess had orchestrated her own kidnapping and would make the first helpless prince she met her pawn.

Lily hopped closer, searching for the amulet. And there it was, dangling from a lamp adorned with gilded leaves and roses, atop a mauve nightstand next to the bed. She took another hop then stopped. It was too easy. This must be a trap. The princess must have hung her prize in such an obvious place to trick a potential thief. But what thief could manage to sneak past the dragon and into this room?

She dug under the soft carpet and tossed a handful of dust at the lamp. If something invisible was hidden around the stand, it would be covered in dirt. Nothing appeared.

She had only learned the spells required for her potions. Crocus showed an aptitude for magic, but Lily lacked the required patience. She couldn't fail now. She'd have to risk it. She bent her long, strong legs and leaped onto the dresser. From there it was an easy hop to the lamp. The amulet was dangling from a gilded leaf on the lamp base. Lily stretched her arm, trying to grab it, but she was too far away. Splinter was strapped to her back. Would the blade be long enough to reach the amulet? She pulled it from its sheath and extended it as far as she could, using the tip to knock the amulet onto the floor.

"Yes!" she grunted in celebration and leaped back onto the dresser.

The instant the chain hit the carpet, the lamp began to shiver and shake. More leaves sprouted from the base, creating arms and legs. Two decorative roses glowed like angry red eyes. In the space of a few seconds, a creature made of gilded leaves and roses glowered in the darkness, searching for the intruder. Lily hid behind a stack of books, blessing her small size. The enchanted creature couldn't see her.

"Thorn, what's the matter?" Princess Belinda mumbled as the monster lamp growled louder. She slid from the bed, picked up the amulet, and slipped it over her head.

"Did you hear a little intruder?" she crooned, speaking to the lamp as if it were a pet. "Be a good boy. Find me the little thief and capture it for me."

Lily kept still as the lamp sniffed the room, whining.

"I knew that spell would come in handy," Princess Belinda laughed.

"Come on out," her velvet voice slithered through the cavern. "You can't hide from me."

The lamp stiffened and darted from the room. Lily sighed in relief. Whatever it had sensed, at least she was safe for the moment.

Then a scream echoed through the tunnels and Lily's heart leaped to her throat.

"Let me go! Let me go!" Cassie was shouting.

Lily's heart sank. Cassie had come to rescue her, but she had put the quest in danger.

CHAPTER 13

TRUE LOVE'S KISS

Cassie kicked and punched as the leafy lamp monster clutched the back of her cloak.

"Let me go!" she repeated as she dug in her bag of supplies for one of Lily's concoctions. But before she could find anything helpful, she saw the emboldened dragon and the angry princess running toward her at full speed.

Princess Belinda pointed a finger at Cassie.

"Incinerate her!" she commanded.

"As you wish, princess." Ignis the dragon took a deep breath, preparing to spew fire.

"Incinerate this!" Cassie whipped a stink sphere from her bag and tossed it to the ground, where it cracked, enveloping Ignis, Princess Belinda, and the leafy lamp monster in a foul cloud.

"Gah! What is that?" Ignis gagged as he inhaled a lungful of the stench.

"Burn her!" Princess Belinda choked, her violet eyes watering as she held a lace-trimmed handkerchief to her nose.

"Yes, princess," Ignis wheezed. He tried to inhale again and choked. A flame shot over Princess Belinda's head, singeing her hair and narrowly missing Cassie. The leaf monster wasn't so lucky. As the flame melted one of its arms and half its torso, it squealed piteously and dropped Cassie.

"You fool," Princess Belinda groaned as she gathered her fire-damaged hair. "You can't hit one measly girl?"

Ignis glared at the princess. "Would you like to try?"

Princess Belinda curled her fingers around the amulet hanging from her neck. "Careful, Ignis, that almost sounded like insolence."

The dragon winced, struggling to look the princess in the eye. He was forced to obey her every order. Lily's heart swelled with pity.

"Cassie. Psst. Cassie. Over here."

As Ignis bowed his massive dragon head in submission, Cassie scrambled to Lily's hiding place behind a forest of stalagmites.

"I am your humble servant, princess," Ignis murmured, but fury glinted in his eyes.

Princess Belinda nodded. "Good. Now get that..." She looked around but Cassie was gone. "Find her, you two fools!" she screeched.

Ignis hurried toward the maze of tunnels, and Thorn, the poor leaf monster, hobbled behind him. They ran past Cassie and Lily, who were hiding in the shadows, not daring to breathe.

"Once they leave, we'll get the amulet," Cassie whispered. "She won't be able to control the dragon once we steal it."

"No, *I* need to get the amulet," Lily corrected her. "*You* need to get out of here. It's too dangerous."

"I'm not leaving without you," Cassie said.

"You didn't train most of your life for this mission," Lily snapped.

"Neither did you," Cassie retorted.

Lily tried to think of a response. "I'm better at this than you are."

"Actually," A third voice floated over their heads. "I don't think either of you is very good at your mission."

They looked up to see Princess Belinda levitating over them, a smug smile on her face, her hands glowing.

"Sometimes it's best to do the work yourself." The princess pointed a delicate finger, releasing a bolt of light. Cassie grabbed Lily and dove to the right. The stalagmite they'd been hiding behind shattered into pieces as she ran.

"Head for the exit!" Lily shouted, and Cassie sprinted for the cavern opening.

Princess Belinda was in hot pursuit, floating over the stone passageway, her singed hair and nightgown fluttering around her.

"Wilfred never mentioned that the princess could do magic,"

Cassie panted as she ran.

"Wilfred probably didn't do more than minimal research." Lily saw that the princess was preparing another fireball. "Go left."

Cassie dodged left. The fireball struck the cavern wall so forcefully rocks cascaded around them.

"He seemed to focus on discovering how dangerous the dragon is," Lily said.

At that moment Ignis appeared before them in a blur of red light, blocking the exit.

"Go right," Lily ordered.

Cassie obeyed, but Thorn appeared, blocking their path.

"As I said before, you're not very good at this." Princess Belinda hovered behind them.

"You are nothing more than an ordinary villain," Lily snapped.

"Excuse me?" Princess Belinda's eyes glowed brighter. "I am far from ordinary. Look at me." She spread her creamy arms wide. "I am known as a pretty damsel in distress, waiting to be rescued by the prince who will carry her off on his steed to a fairytale happily ever after. And yet." She paused, her hand still glowing. "I am so much more than that." She eyed Lily and Cassie with distaste. "Do you know the secret of the Kingdom of Lamia?"

"That all its citizens are two-faced witches?" Lily guessed.

The flames glowing from the tips of Princess Belinda's fingers grew brighter. "That we have been secretly cultivating the magical arts for centuries."

"Which is precisely what I said," Lily pointed out.

Princess Belinda stomped her foot and her pretty face twisted into a pout. "You loathsome little amphibian! You have failed to understand. I have trained for years, studied spells and magic. I researched the dragons I could exploit in order to plan my own kidnapping."

"Oh, Iggy," Lily taunted the dragon. "Do you enjoy being the least dangerous dragon on earth?"

Ignis glowered, a growl rumbling in his throat.

"I am speaking!" Princess Belinda snapped. "I have studied. I have planned. I would be betrothed to a prince in line for the throne. But within a year, a plague would sweep across the kingdom. The people would be ill, dying, desperate."

Cassie interrupted, "And you alone would possess the cure?"

"Which I would bestow only on subjects who accepted me as their queen."

"And those who refused to bow down to you would die? You don't deserve to rule," Lily declared.

"Oh, but I do." The light in the princess's eyes glowed green, and a golden hue surrounded her tattered body. "I deserve to be a queen, a goddess, a savior to my people."

"You deserve to be a slug," Lily taunted.

"Silence, loathsome amphibian! I have tired of speaking." Princess Belinda aimed another energy blast at Lily and Cassie. "I must ready myself for my prince."

Time seemed to slow. Seconds became minutes. Lily saw the magic moving toward her and reached for Splinter, but it was already out of its sheath and in Cassie's hands.

The blade grew back to its original size as Cassie wielded it. The energy ricocheted off the blade, hitting Princess Belinda square in the chest, and sending her careening into a wall.

"You little brats!" the princess stammered as she staggered to her feet. With her singed hair and ashen nightgown, she resembled an evil witch, her beautiful face twisted in anger. "You will pay for that!"

The princess lifted her hand once more, then stopped, dumbstruck. The amulet was emitting its own light, and as the rays grew, cracks appeared in the gem and widened.

"No!" she shouted, clawing the chain from her neck, her eyes wild. "I will be a queen. A savior." The chain caught in her hair, and before she could tug it free, an enormous force knocked everyone off their feet.

As they were hurled past falling stalagmites and nearly being impaled, Lily could feel that Cassie was shielding her with her body. They hit the ground with a thud, and Cassie rolled over twice before coming to a stop. Lily wriggled free of her friend's embrace.

"Cassie," Lily hopped up to her face. "Are you all right?"

Cassie's beautiful almond-shaped eyes fluttered. "I don't know," she groaned. "I can't feel my toes."

"Don't move, I'll check you for injuries." Lily hopped down to Cassie's feet. There were a few cuts and scrapes, and her skirt was ripped, but she didn't see anything serious until something caught her eye. She gasped. A gooey orange substance was bubbling and oozing from Cassie's feet and legs.

"Yuck! What is this?" Cassie cried, as she sat up and tried to brush it away. The goo spread to her fingers, covering her hands in seconds.

"Don't fret. I'll help you." Lily's mind raced. Something in her pouch might help.

"No," Cassie ordered. "Don't touch it. You'll just end up like me."

The orange sludge continued to ooze. It had reached Cassie's waist and was hardening into a heavy, rock-like substance.

"Cassie, I can't leave you like this." Tears stung Lily's eyes.

"You have no choice," Cassie's insisted through tears of her own. "If this goo covers you, you'll be as useless as I am."

"I'll find a way to remove it," Lily promised. "I'll come back for you, then we'll return to Frogville together."

"I'd like that." Cassie gave her little green friend a weak smile. The goo had reached her neck. Only her arms and head were free. "Lily, I know I'm not a prince, but I want to thank you for everything. For being my friend."

She scooped Lily up and planted a kiss on her tiny head.

Lily's body was immersed in light. Her limbs tingled and ached, and she felt like she was being stretched like taffy. Cassie was shrinking and so was the cavern. Cassie no longer towered over the little frog. They were the same size.

Lily looked down and saw her familiar fingers and toes, her arms and legs. She was herself again. She was free.

"Cassie! Cassie, look! I'm back. I'm…" but as Lily turned she saw that her friend had become a statue. "Cassie?" Lily touched the cool, smooth surface. She could see Cassie within the stone, her eyes open and staring but unresponsive. Her body looked as though it were encased in amber, her features frozen in a silent plea for help.

"No, no, no!" Lily beat her fists on the hard surface until her knuckles ached. She snatched a rock and pounded on the hardened substance but failed to cause so much as a crack. Splinter was lying a few feet away. She grabbed the sword and tried hacking at the stone, but the amber casing was too hard.

Princess Belinda started this, Lily thought. She stumbled through the crumbled rocks and stalagmites, her legs wobbly from having been enchanted for so long. Being able to run again felt bizarre, as she zigzagged through waist-high rock piles that had towered over her head minutes before. She vaulted a small crevice that had seemed like a canyon and stopped short.

She was facing three more statues. Thorn, Ignis, and Princess Belinda were all encased in amber, trapped, frozen in their final struggle.

"Snail slime!" Lily cursed in frustration. How could she save her friend? "It's not fair," she whispered, clenching her fists. A tear ran down one cheek. As she brushed it away, the grass bracelet Asphodel had made for her scratched her face. She was exhausted, too weak to stand. Her knees buckled and she collapsed to the ground.

"It's not fair. It's not fair," she repeated, as more tears fell. Soon she was encased in a warm, flower-scented breeze.

"What's not fair, my dear?" Asphodel was standing next to her, leaning on a cane of rough-hewn oak.

Lily pointed at the amber figures. "I was finally free from my curse. Why did this happen?"

Asphodel regarded the statues, and her face softened. "Ah. The Domini Vindictae."

"The what?" Lily was so tired, she had to force the question from her throat.

"The spell that was put on the dragon's amulet is known as the Domini Vindictae. You might consider it a revenge charm, inflicted by anyone who tries to destroy his power. The magic is meant to attach itself to those near him, trapping them for eternity."

"Eternity?" Another tear rolled down Lily's cheek. "So Cassie will be imprisoned in stone forever?"

"Cassie?" Asphodel frowned and squinted at the three statues. "Which one is she?"

"She's none of these. She's there." Lily led Asphodel to her friend. "The force hurled us here. She protected me with her body."

"And gave you the kiss of true love, as well," Asphodel murmured. She shrugged as Lily stared at her in surprise. "Anyone who cares enough to protect you in such a way has the power to free you from your curse."

Lily touched the top of her head where Cassie had kissed her. "If I care for her too, can I free her, as well?"

Without waiting for a response, she knelt next to her friend and kissed the smooth stone over her forehead. Nothing happened.

"The Domini Vindictae requires a more difficult antidote."

Lily turned to look at the old woman. "But there is one, isn't there?"

Asphodel hesitated, then nodded. "Yes. Over the Mountains of Cinis there is a fountain. The Fountain of Somnia. If you collect some of the water and sprinkle it on your friend, she will be freed."

"Very well." Lily got to her feet. "Please draw a map of this place. I'll go there now and bring it back."

"It's very dangerous," Asphodel warned.

"I will go, just the same."

"Few people have ever survived the journey."

"I... don't...care," Lily repeated. "She's my friend, and she risked her life to free me. I owe it to her to return the favor."

"You could simply return to your home," Asphodel suggested. "You've freed your entire village from the curse. I'm sure you would be given a hero's welcome."

Lily shook her head. "I can't go back, not yet. I made a promise to Cassie that I would take her home with me. I don't break promises."

Asphodel's face softened and she smiled. "True love in its

most potent form," she murmured. With a snap of her fingers, a map floated into Lily's hands. "You'll find the safest route marked," she said. "I wish you the best of luck and success on your quest." Her fingers tightened on Lily's shoulder. "Be careful," Asphodel said. "And thank you for releasing the wizard from his curse."

Lily tucked the map into her pouch. "I'll do my best to be careful." She looked Asphodel in the eye, "And you're welcome."

Lily knelt beside Cassie once again. "I'll come back for you," she whispered, although she was sure that her friend couldn't hear her. "I'll get the water and we'll go back to Frogville together."

Lily stood, wiping one last tear from her eye. She looked at Asphodel. "Would it be at all possible for you to protect her while I'm away?"

Asphodel nodded. She dragged her oak stick in the dirt, creating a circle around Cassie's body. With a snap of her fingers and a few whispered words, a protective bubble appeared around the imprisoned girl. "That's the best I can do. Only you can open this bubble. The touch of your hand will crack it."

Lily sighed with relief. "Thank you."

Asphodel offered a wizened hand and Lily clasped it. "No. Thank you," the old woman said. "Now that the wizard is free, I can rest in peace."

Lily attempted a smile. "Well, I'm off," she said, striding

towards the opening of the cavern. She paused and looked back to say goodbye, but Asphodel was gone.

The early morning sun warmed Lily's face. She squinted and pulled her hood over her head to protect herself from the desert heat, then walked away with renewed determination. The first stop on her journey: the Fountain of Somnia.

She found no sign of Prince Raymond or his soldiers. The smoke had cleared and the scent of blooming roses filled the air. The only sound she heard was the chirping of birds.

The curse had been lifted, but joy was far from Lily's heart. Cassie's tomb awaited. As she headed toward the mountains, she scanned the salty terrain for a certain prince with unpaid favors. Lily's new quest was underway.

ABOUT THE AUTHOR

Sharla J. Frost grew up in Frogville, Oklahoma. She went to law school, practiced law, then retired back home to raise cattle and write books. She is the former President of Litigation Counsel of America and an active member of the National Association of Women Lawyers. Today, most of her days are spent herding cats and cows. She thinks dragons are simply frogs who have grown wings and flown away. Oh, yes. Children are her favorite people in the world.